CLA...
CHANCE TO SHINE

Written by Rachael Wong
Illustrated by Vivienne Husband

BREWIN BOOKS

First published by
Brewin Books Ltd, 56 Alcester Road,
Studley, Warwickshire B80 7LG in 2017
www.brewinbooks.com

© Text: Rachael Wong, 2017
© Illustrations: Vivienne Husband, 2017

Front and rear inside cover illustrations by
pupils of Bentley Heath C of E Primary School.

ISBN: 978-1-85858-560-4

A Cataloguing in Publication Record
for this title is available from the British Library.

Typeset in Agmena Pro Book
Printed in Great Britain by
Hobbs The Printers Ltd.

Contents

Foreword by Moeen Ali

"I have been an England cricketer for many years and have played all over the world. Just like you I started playing cricket in the playground at school! Some of the best times I have had have been meeting young people like you through Chance to Shine. I see for myself the fun you all have, the great exercise you get and all the other important things you learn about, like being brave and playing fair, working in teams and learning to win and lose well. Not everyone gets the chance to play this game that I love, so I hope that you enjoy this story about a group of friends just like you and your class, and I also hope it encourages you to keep playing and enjoying cricket. It can help you learn a lot about life, so play with a big smile on your face and always try your best!"

CHANCE TO SHINE
Spreading the power of cricket

All royalties from this book will be given directly to
Chance to Shine, registered charity number 1123385.

Introduction

Chance to Shine is a national charity on a mission to spread the power of cricket throughout schools and communities. We take cricket to new places and use it to ignite new passions, teach vital skills, unite diverse groups and educate young people from Cornwall to Cardiff to County Durham.

Over three million boys and girls in nearly 12,000 state schools have played and learned through cricket thanks to the Chance to Shine Schools programme. More than 600,000 children enter the state school system each year and with this our work goes on, to offer all boys and girls their chance to shine.

To find out more about our programmes, please visit: www.chancetoshine.org

Chapter 1

Alex grabbed his school bag and ran out of the front door. He was so excited! Today was the day he had been waiting for; the Chance to Shine cricket coaches were coming into his school. Alex loved cricket and he was looking forward to playing it with his school friends. Most of them had never played cricket before and he was desperate to show his friends what fun cricket could be. Alex hoped they would then come down to his local club and join his Under 9's team.

"Come on, mum, why are you so *slow*?" asked Alex impatiently as mum locked the door. "Let's get to school quickly so I can talk to my friends about Chance to Shine cricket before the bell goes."

Mum smiled, put the key in her pocket, and tried to catch up with Alex. He was already halfway down the road!

Chapter 2

Alex and his friends always found each other in the playground before school each morning. Omaris, Flo, Jaya, and Jake were already there. Alex rushed up to them, breathless from his high speed walk to school. "Are you all looking forward to Chance to Shine cricket today?" he asked everyone.

"A bit," shrugged Omaris.

"Sort of," said Flo.

"Maybe," answered Jaya.

"Is it?" asked Jake.

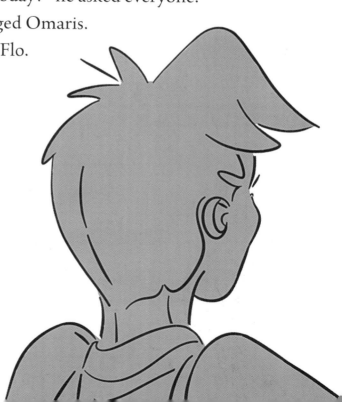

The school bell rang. "Come on, guys, it's going to be great," insisted Alex as they all got into line. The other children giggled – Alex just loved cricket!

Mrs Kelly, their teacher, walked down the line. "No talking children, please," she said. Class 10 started walking into school one by one. Mrs Kelly sighed as Alex walked past her: she knew it was going to be a long morning for young Alex.

Chapter 3

The afternoon finally came. Class 10 were already changed into their PE kits when Mo and Nadia, the Chance to Shine coaches, arrived at school. "Good afternoon, Class 10," they said, as they put down their heavy bags of equipment on the playground. "Are we ready to play some cricket?"

"Yes," said Alex eagerly, jumping up and down in excitement.

"A bit," shrugged Omaris.

"Sort of," said Flo.

"Maybe," answered Jaya.

"Are we?" asked Jake.

"Yes, we are," said Nadia, smiling at Jake. Then, turning to the other children, she continued, "And next month you are all going to be playing in a cricket festival against the other schools in the area."

Nadia then got Class 10 warmed up with a fun game called 'Volcanoes', where the children ran around

picking balls off cones and then finding an empty cone to put the ball back down on. Alex buzzed around like a wasp at a picnic on a hot day, picking up and putting down.

"Right," said Mo, "Now we are going to do some catching. Get into pairs, everyone. Remember to stand with your feet shoulder width apart, knees bent, hands together and fingers pointing down. And make sure you WATCH the ball."

Despite Mo's very clear instructions, the catching practice did not go well. Nobody, apart from Alex, could catch.

Next came some batting practice. Alex watched in despair as his classmates swung their bats at ball after ball and missed nearly all of them. Worse still, the balls were on cones – they weren't even moving!

Chapter 4

At home time, Alex was the last to pack his school bag. As he trudged sadly out of the classroom, Mrs Kelly could tell how disappointed he was. "Cheer up, Alex", said Mrs Kelly. "The Chance to Shine lesson next week might go much better."

"I don't think so," said Alex. He looked down at the floor and poked one of the chairs with his foot. "I really want my friends to like cricket and come to play at my club, but I didn't think they would be this hopeless."

"Mmm, let's think about this," suggested Mrs Kelly. "What helped *you* become better at cricket, Alex?" she asked.

"Well", answered Alex a little hesitantly, "When I was little, my mum told me the story of Lord Morvidus, who was the ancient lord of the Britons. He was attacked by a fierce giant while he was riding in the forest one day. The giant knocked him off his horse

and Morvidus lost his sword as he fell. The only weapon Morvidus could find was a tree. He was incredibly strong and managed to pull the tree out of the ground to use it as a weapon and win the fight against the giant. Mum said that if I could be as brave, strong and resilient as Morvidus then I would be just fine when I went out to bat."

"And did it work?" enquired Mrs Kelly.

"Definitely! I hit the ball all the way to the boundary," replied Alex. "Quite a few times," he added, a little more cheerfully.

Mrs Kelly had listened carefully to Alex's story. She shared his disappointment. She too wanted the class to enjoy the cricket festival. "You go home now, Alex," she told him, "and leave this with me…."

Mrs Kelly was beginning to have an idea.

Chapter 5

The following week, Class 10 assembled on the playground again for their Chance to Shine lesson. "Hello everyone," said Mo. "Now, before we start, Nadia and I would like to introduce a special guest who is going to help us with our lesson today."

"Wicked," said Omaris to his friends. "My cousin said a really famous cricket player called Moeen Ali came to his school. I bet it's him. My cousin says he's AMAZING."

At that moment Mrs Kelly appeared, accompanied by a tall man dressed in a full suit of armour and a long cape, and carrying a very big stick. The children all stared in complete amazement. All except Omaris, who jumped up in outrage. "Hey, that's not Moeen Ali," he shouted. "My cousin has a photo of him and he doesn't look like that. That's not fair!"

"Oh come on Omaris, sit down, he's still pretty cool," said Flo. "Even if he looks as if he's going to be as rubbish as us at cricket," she giggled.

"Hang on, I know who he is," shouted Alex, now taking a turn to jump up and down. "He's Lord Morvidus."

"Correct, young man," said the knight, with a twinkle in his eye. "Now, let's get on with the lesson, shall we?"

Mo and Nadia emptied their bags and prepared the warm up. This was going to be one of the most interesting Chance to Shine sessions they had ever done!

Chapter 6

For the next hour, Morvidus clunked around the playground in his armour, roaring encouragement to the children, and hitting balls with his long stick whenever he could. He hit one ball and it flew right over the school, landing in the infants' playground! Even Omaris was impressed: perhaps this guy wasn't so bad after all.

When Mo and Nadia left at the end of the lesson, Morvidus sat down with the children and told them the story of how he had fought the giant in the forest with nothing more than a tree he had pulled out of the ground. "I never gave up," he told Class 10, "and neither should you. Now, in three weeks you have a cricket festival against other schools. What are you going to do before then to get ready for it?"

Omaris was keen to make up for being a bit rude to Morvidus earlier on. "I'm going to practise catching by throwing the ball against my garage

wall," he announced.

"Great idea," said Flo. "Can I come round to yours and do that too?"

Before Omaris even had time to nod, Jaya had shouted out, "And I'm going to play cricket with my brothers to improve my batting."

"Me too," said Jake.

Everyone looked at Jake.

"You haven't got any brothers!" laughed Jaya. "But you can come and join in at our house."

Alex was so proud of his friends. At the end of school that day, Alex went to speak to Mrs Kelly. "That was great fun thanks, Mrs Kelly, but may I ask, who was Lord Morvidus in real life?"

"He's called Chris, and he's my next door neighbour," chuckled Mrs Kelly. "Chris is an actor and every summer he works as a knight at a big castle nearby. He also plays cricket so he was really happy to come along and help today. Don't you think he makes a great Lord Morvidus?"

"He's brilliant," agreed Alex. "Thanks Mrs Kelly," he added as he hurried happily out of the classroom door, eager to tell mum everything that had happened.

Chapter 7

Three weeks later, Class 10 set out from school to their local cricket club for the Chance to Shine cricket festival. Alex's club coach Tom had told him he was going to come down and support them. Mo and Nadia were there too, organising everything, and were pleased to see Class 10. They were really impressed with how much Alex's class had improved over the last few weeks.

Class 10 was going to be split into two teams for the cricket festival. Luckily, Mrs Kelly had made sure that Alex and his friends were all on the same team. She too was very pleased how hard the group of friends had worked to improve.

The friends didn't let Mrs Kelly down. All day, each of the children tried their hardest in every game and remembered everything that the coaches had told them. They also remembered what Morvidus had told them – Never Give Up! Best of all, they encouraged each other and worked together as a team. Mrs Kelly was very proud.

In each match, the team who were fielding had their accompanying adult to bowl for them. As the day went on, everyone noticed there was an adult with one of the other teams who was bowling demon balls that were impossible to hit. They either came at 90 miles an hour towards your tummy, or they trickled along the floor and somehow found their way between your legs and onto the stumps. The lady bowling these impossible balls was wearing very bright pink trainers and a matching pink jacket with shiny pink sequins on it. Everyone was talking about

'the pink lady'. "That's not fair," grumbled Mrs Kelly, "She shouldn't be bowling like that when all the other adults are being fair."

The morning rounds of matches were over. Before everyone settled down for their packed lunches, Nadia announced which two teams had done well enough to play in the final after lunch. Alex's team went wild when theirs was the first team to be called out for the final. But then they all groaned when they heard they would be playing against High Castle School and the lady with the pink trainers! Alex also knew that five of the boys and two of the girls in the High Castle team all played for his club's local rivals. Somehow they had all been put in the same school team. This was going to be a very difficult match to win.

Chapter 8

"Alex", said a voice behind him. Alex turned round and saw his club coach Tom walking towards him and his friends. "I've been watching your team all morning," continued Tom. "You and your friends can win this final. You can catch well, bat well, and you all play together as a team. That High Castle team spent half of their last match arguing about who was going to bat first. Then they spent the rest of the match arguing about who was fielding where."

"Really?" said Alex, suddenly feeling more positive.

"Yes, really," replied Tom. "And after this festival, whatever the result in the final, I hope your friends come down to the cricket club for junior training night. You will all do really well in our Under 9's teams."

"Wow, yes please," said Omaris.

"Wicked," shouted Flo.

"Yes!" exclaimed Jaya.

"And me?" asked Jake.

"Yes! And you, Jake!" shouted everyone.

Alex grinned like a cat with a big bowl of cream. Then he remembered something. "What about the lady in the pink trainers?" he asked Tom.

"Well," said Tom, winking at Alex, "I think Mo and Nadia have worked that one out. Eat your lunch and we'll see what happens."

Chapter 9

Alex and his friends jumped for joy when Nadia announced, just before the final, that Mo would be bowling to both teams to make sure everyone faced the same kind of bowling. The lady in the pink trainers looked very angry. So did the High Castle team.

Now it was all down to Alex and his team. They were batting first. There were no arguments; everyone knew that Alex should be the first to bat. Remembering the story of Morvidus, he launched several balls way beyond the fielders and then ran like a rabbit between the stumps. Alex's team mates cheered and cheered.

Each of them then took their turn to bat. Poor Jake was bowled out first ball, but then recovered himself to score a few runs. Flo then scored a few too, and so did Omaris – but then he was run out, so that meant some runs would be deducted. Last to bat was Jaya. She was very nervous but made herself feel better by remembering all the practice she had done with her brothers. And the practice paid off – Jaya hit the first ball so hard that it went over onto the next pitch where the third and fourth placed teams were playing.

Alex's team had scored 62 runs at the end of their innings, once the runs for lost wickets were deducted. The High Castle team was very confident, though. "That lot can't catch," Alex heard them saying. Alex really hoped they weren't right. To be fair, it was really only Jake who was a bit hopeless at catching.

Flo chased around the field after balls like a puppy, but the High Castle team kept scoring runs. Alex was worried they were getting close to his team's score. Mrs Kelly was looking nervous too.

The final ball was about to be bowled. Alex knew that High Castle were just ahead on runs. That meant Alex's team *had* to take a wicket so that High Castle

would have runs taken off their current total. The
batsman hit the ball right up in the air and it started to
come down in Jake's direction. Jake stood still as the
ball came towards him. Everyone froze. The
ball seemed to be falling in slow motion.
Suddenly, Jake lifted his hands way
above his head. The ball landed in
Jake's left hand and then bounced up in
the air again! Alex could hardly watch.
Quickly, Jake brought his hands together
and, as the ball fell for the second time into his
hands, he closed his fingers around it and held it tight.
JAKE HAD CAUGHT THE BALL! Moments later, he
was buried under his team-mates as they all jumped on
top of him to celebrate. Mrs Kelly laughed and then
shouted, "Jake, how did you manage to catch that ball
– *with your eyes closed?!*"

Chapter 10

Alex's team had won! Everyone was delighted. Coach Tom was very excited, "Our Under 9's teams will be invincible this season," he shouted. Mrs Kelly rang Chris from her mobile phone and all the children crowded round to tell him the news.

Luckily, it was his afternoon tea break at the castle, but it still took him a long time to find his phone under all his armour.

"Well done, everyone," Chris roared down the phone when he heard they had won. "You've done brilliantly. But more importantly, did you have fun?"

"Yes, we did," shouted Alex.

"Of course," said Omaris.

"You bet," screamed Flo.

"Too right," agreed Jaya.

"It was AMAZING!" yelled Jake.

THE END

Remember, this is a story, so there will be no lady in pink trainers demon bowling at you in your Chance to Shine sessions!

If you enjoyed this story about Alex and Morvidus, you might also like to read 'Legend of Morvidus', written by Rachael Wong and illustrated by Jim Troughton.